Hannah was staring into one of the pens. On the other side of the railings was a ball of fluffy white and blue-grey fur. It was love at first sight.

"Hello, puppy," Hannah whispered.

At the sound of her voice the puppy sat up and yawned, showing his big pink tongue. Hannah giggled. The puppy's markings made him look as if he was wearing goggles around his piercing blue eyes. He was the cutest thing she'd ever seen.

The puppy's furry ears pricked up and he gambolled over to the front of the pen, wagging his long feathery tail.

"His feet look too big for him," Hannah murmured, enchanted. She bent down and flattened her hand against the railings. The puppy licked at her fingers and wagged his tail furiously.

Hannah glanced pleadingly at her parents. They were smiling from ear to ear, and so was Ellie.

"Awww, he's sooooo adorable!" Ellie gushed.

Have you read all these books in the
Battersea Dogs &
Cats Home series?

BATTERSEA DOGS & CATS HOME

HUEY'S
story

by
Jane Clarke

Illustrated by Sharon Rentta
Puzzle illustrations by Jason Chapman

RED FOX

BATTERSEA DOGS AND CATS HOME: HUEY'S STORY
A RED FOX BOOK 978 1 849 41415 9

First published in Great Britain by Red Fox,
an imprint of Random House Children's Books
A Random House Group Company

This edition published 2011

1 3 5 7 9 10 8 6 4 2

The Random House Group Limited supports The Forest Stewardship Council
(FSC), the leading international forest certification organisation. All our titles
that are printed on Greenpeace approved FSC certified paper carry the FSC
logo. Our paper procurement policy can be found at:
www.randomhouse.co.uk/environment

Mixed Sources
Product group from well-managed
forests and other controlled sources
www.fsc.org Cert no. TT-COC-002139
© 1996 Forest Stewardship Council
FSC

Set in 13/20 Stone Informal

Red Fox Books are published by Random House Children's Books,
61–63 Uxbridge Road, London W5 5SA

www.**kids**at**randomhouse**.co.uk
www.**randomhouse**.co.uk

Addresses for companies within The Random House Group Limited
can be found at: www.randomhouse.co.uk/offices.htm

THE RANDOM HOUSE GROUP Limited Reg. No. 954009

A CIP catalogue record for this book is available from the British Library.

Printed and bound in Great Britain by
CPI Bookmarque, Croydon, CR0 4TD

**Turn to page 93 for lots
of information on
Battersea Dogs & Cats Home,
plus some cool activities!**

Meet the stars of the Battersea Dogs & Cats Home series to date . . .

Bailey

Misty

Chester

Rusty

Max

Daisy

Snowy

Stella

Huey

Angel

Cosmo

The Newcomer

Seven-year-old Hannah Cole blushed as beetroot-red as her new school uniform. It was her first day at East Oak Primary School and everyone in Year Three Acorn Class was staring at her!

Hannah crossed her fingers behind her back. *Be my new friends*, she wished as Miss Reynolds introduced her.

"Hannah and her mum and dad and

big sister Ellie have moved down from
Manchester to be closer to their
grandpa," Miss Reynolds told the class.
"Acorns, give Hannah a warm welcome!"

Acorn Class clapped politely as
Hannah walked past the paired desks to
an empty place in the back row.

A friendly-looking girl with a long
brown ponytail and freckles
grinned at Hannah as
she sat down. "My
name's Louise,"
she told her.

"Hi." Hannah smiled back happily.
She'd been so sad to leave her old friends
behind in Manchester, but here she was,
making a new friend right away, just like
Mum and Dad said she would!

Whoosh! Something whizzed through
the air and hit Hannah on the arm.
It was only a paper plane, but
it really stung. Hannah
looked for the
culprit.

A girl in the front
row with short, fair hair
was scowling furiously at her.
Hannah's smile faded.

"That's my best
friend, Gemma,"
Louise hissed,
grabbing the
paper plane and
shoving it under
the desk before Miss
Reynolds noticed. Louise unfolded the
paper plane and looked at the writing
on it.

Hannah glanced over. It said: CU @
break in pencil.

"Gemma usually sits
next to me," Louise
whispered, "but
Miss Reynolds
splits us up for
maths. She says
we get more work
done that way."

"No talking, now, Acorns," Miss
Reynolds told the class. "It's
time to concentrate."

Miss Reynolds
tried to make
maths fun, but
Hannah
couldn't help
noticing that
Gemma kept
twisting round
and glowering at
her. Hopefully
they'd *all* become
friends at break, she thought.

At last the bell rang.

"Can I play with you?" Hannah asked
Louise as they dashed out of the
classroom into the playground, but before
Louise could reply, Gemma ran up.

Gemma stuck her tongue out at
Hannah and linked arms with Louise.
Louise glanced apologetically over her
shoulder as Gemma marched her away.
Poor Hannah was left standing in the
middle of the playground. All around her,
children were laughing and giggling and
racing around, having fun. Hannah

looked on longingly. She was really good
at skipping and tag, but no one thought
to ask her to join in.

The rest of the day seemed to take
for ever. Louise and Gemma were allowed
to sit next to each other in the other
lessons, so Hannah had to sit on her own
at the front.

"How was your first day at school?" Dad asked that evening as the Cole family sat round the table eating dinner.

Hannah's fifteen-year-old sister, Ellie, swept her hair out of her eyes.

"I fit right in!" she announced between mouthfuls of pasta. "The girls are really nice, the boys are cute and we get to chill out in the common room between classes and play our own music! What's not to like? The teachers are OK, too."

Hannah's mother and father looked at each other in relief.

"How about you, Hannah?" Mum asked. Hannah pushed her food around her plate.

"It's not like you to be so quiet." Mum exchanged a worried look with Dad. "Come on, love," she coaxed. "How was East Oak Primary?"

Hannah shrugged her shoulders. "Fine," she said at last.

It was
hard to fall asleep
that night. Hannah got up
and stared down from her bedroom
window into the long walled garden of
the new house. It would be a brilliant
garden for a dog, she thought. But when
they were living in Manchester, she'd
asked and asked Mum and Dad if she
could have a puppy, and they'd said "no"
again and again and again.

Hannah sighed as she closed the curtains and got back into bed. She missed her old life in Manchester so much.

Will I ever find a friend in London? she wondered.

A Good Move

Hannah stood at the school gates, looking forlorn. It was Friday afternoon at last, the end of the first week of school, and she still hadn't made a proper friend. She didn't have anyone of her own age to play with over the weekend.

"Bye, Hannah!" Louise ran past, closely followed by Gemma.

"Bye, Louise!" A ghost of a smile lit up

Hannah's face, but it
was swiftly crushed
by the glare
Gemma gave her.

"Who was that
nice girl?" Mum
asked, rushing up. "One
of your new friends?"

"That's Louise," Hannah said. "She's
lovely. But she already
has a best friend
called Gemma,
and Gemma
doesn't like
me at all." A
tear dripped
down
Hannah's
cheek.

"Everyone's happy with the friends they've got," she sobbed. "They don't need me! All my friends are in Manchester . . ."

"Cheer up, love." Mum gave Hannah a hug. "It's just taking a bit of time to settle in, that's all. You'll make new friends soon." She handed Hannah a tissue. "Your dad and I have some plans for the weekend, so you won't be lonely."

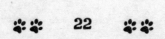

"What plans?" Hannah snuffled, blowing her nose. But Mum wouldn't tell Hannah what the plans were, and she wouldn't tell Ellie, either.

"I've been invited to watch a movie with a bunch of my new friends," Ellie announced at breakfast on Saturday. "So whatever it is we're doing today, I hope we'll be back in time."

"We will," Mum reassured her. She exchanged a glance with Dad.

"We thought you might like to take a trip to Battersea," Dad said, tipping crunchy cereal into Hannah's bowl.

"Battersea?" Ellie looked puzzled.

"What's at Batter-sea?" Hannah asked, pouring milk on her cereal and taking a mouthful.

"Is there a beach?"

"Battersea's a part of London," Dad explained.

"There's no beach, but there is a very famous animal rescue centre called Battersea Dogs & Cats Home. They take in unwanted and lost dogs and cats and do their best to find them new homes . . ."

Hannah stopped crunching and held her breath.

"We thought you might be interested in meeting some of the dogs who live there," Dad went on, "so we made an appointment at the Home."

"Moving here is a new start for all of us," Mum added with a smile, "and this house has such a big garden, we think we can give a dog a new start in life as well!"

Hannah nearly choked on her breakfast. Coming to London wasn't such a bad move after all!

"Yay!" she spluttered, rushing over to give her mum and dad a hug.

"Dogs are
awesome," Ellie
said slowly, "but
can we choose
one that
doesn't shed
hair all over
my clothes?"

"I'll buy
you a clothes
brush, Ellie
love." Mum
laughed. "Now
you're older, you
won't be spending
as much time at home
as Hannah. So your dad and I thought
that we would ask Hannah to pick out
her perfect pet."

Hannah could hardly believe her ears!

"Me? Choose my very own dog?" She felt as if she was about to burst with excitement. "What are we waiting for?" Hannah squealed, jumping up and down for joy. "Battersea, here we come!"

Finding a New Friend

"Are we nearly there yet?" Hannah asked for the hundredth time. It was hard to sit still in the back seat. Mum and Dad were hopeless with directions and they'd already got lost five times.

"If you ask that again, I'll scream," Ellie informed her as their father made yet another turn.

Mum looked up from the map she had

printed off the computer. "We're here now," she said in relief.

"The Battersea website says they don't have a car park, so this is as close as we can get with the car," Dad agreed, reversing into a parking space on the car-lined street.

Hannah leaped out of the car. "Which way?" she asked, hopping from foot to foot.

"This way." Mum led them down the
road and round the corner, and there
it was.

Hannah's heart jumped for joy as she
read the sign. *Battersea Dogs & Cats Home*.

She raced up to the reception desk.

"'We're here! 'We're here!" she squeaked.

"So I see," the friendly lady on the desk said with a twinkle. She glanced down at the sheet in front of her. "You must be the Cole family. We're expecting you. If you have a seat for a minute or two, someone will come and take you to the kennels."

There was no way Hannah could sit down, but before long a nice man appeared.

"Follow me," he told them, leading them down a corridor. The kennels were full of barking dogs, each in their own separate pen.

"Pooh!" Ellie wrinkled her nose at the smell. "Choose a nice, small, CLEAN dog," she hissed at Hannah.

But Hannah hadn't heard. She was staring into one of the pens. On the

other side of the railings was a ball of fluffy white and blue-grey fur. It was love at first sight.

"Hello, puppy,"
Hannah
whispered.

At the
sound of her
voice the
puppy sat
up and
yawned,
showing his
big pink

tongue. Hannah
giggled. The puppy's markings made him
look as if he was
wearing goggles
around his
piercing blue
eyes. He was the
cutest thing
she'd ever seen.

The puppy's furry ears pricked up and he gambolled over to the front of the pen, wagging his long feathery tail.

"His feet look too big for him," Hannah murmured, enchanted. She bent down and flattened her hand against the railings. The puppy licked at her fingers and wagged his tail furiously.

Hannah glanced pleadingly at her parents. They were smiling from ear to ear, and so was Ellie.

"Awww, he's sooooo adorable!" Ellie gushed.

"He's a very friendly little chap," Dad said.

"His name's Huey," the man from the Home told them. "He's a Siberian husky, about four months old. He was found wandering around the streets without a collar. No one's come to claim him, so he needs a new home."

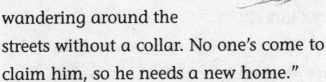

"With us!" Hannah announced immediately.

"Siberian huskies are very special," the man said, a bit doubtfully. "We don't often see them at the Home. They're not a dog for everyone. They are clean . . ."

Hannah glanced triumphantly at Ellie.

". . . and intelligent and very friendly," the man continued. "In fact, they love people so much they are useless guard dogs!"

"We don't need a guard dog," Hannah said quickly.

"This breed of dog gets bored easily," the man said, looking at Hannah's parents. "Huey will need plenty of exercise every day."

"That's OK, I love exercise," Hannah butted in, "and Mum and Dad like long walks, don't you?"

"We do." Mum smiled.

"There's a wild streak in Siberian huskies," the man warned them. "Huey will have to be walked on a lead, or he's likely to run off. And you will need to put a tall fence around your garden to stop him from getting out."

"Our garden already has a high wall around it." Hannah clapped her hands and danced around in a circle. Huey looked at her and wagged his tail so hard it became a blur.

"That's good," the man agreed. "But a husky can make a horrible mess of a garden, you know."

"It's a horrible mess already," Dad laughed, "so that's not a problem."

"Huskies don't often bark," the man went on, "but sometimes they howl like a wolf just for the joy of it – and that can upset the neighbours."

"I've already introduced myself to the neighbours and asked them if they'd mind us having a dog, and they all said they're fine with it," Mum reassured him.

"Then you sound like the right family for a husky," the man said with a smile. "There are some forms to fill in, and next week someone from the Home will visit your house to check it's suitable for Huey. Then you can come and collect him. He's had all his injections so he's ready to go."

Hannah was over the moon!

"Hear that, Huey?" she asked the fluffy
puppy. Huey sat with his head on one
side and gazed at her with sparkling blue
eyes. "In one week, you'll have a new
home – and I'll have a new best friend!"

Exciting Plans

The following Friday, Hannah couldn't wait for school to finish. Gemma had been scowling at her all week, stopping her from making friends with Louise, but nothing could spoil today. The same man they had met at Battersea had come and looked around their house and approved them to be Huey's new owners. Mum and Dad were picking Huey up from Battersea while Hannah was at school!

Hannah stared out of the classroom window. It was like a dream! Yesterday, Grandpa had taken her to the supermarket and she'd chosen some brilliant puppy things like water and food bowls covered in a cute bone design, and a toy ball and squeaky bone. And Mum and Dad had gone to a pet shop and bought Huey a big comfy basket, and a good strong lead to clip onto his Battersea Dogs Home collar.

They were all set! If only school would end!

At last it was the final class of the day.

"Gemma and Louise, you've spent all day chatting to each other," Miss Reynolds announced. "You're giving me a headache. Gemma, change places with Hannah, please, so we can all enjoy a bit of quiet."

Gemma glowered at Hannah as they swapped desks.

"Hi." Louise smiled at Hannah as she sat down. Hannah grinned back.

Miss Reynolds handed out some plain paper.

"Now, I'd like you all to draw a picture and write about what you are going to do this weekend," she instructed the class.

Hannah happily drew a picture of

This weekend I Shall play with Huey

Huey sitting next to his new bowls and his new squeaky ball and toy bone. She wrote underneath it: *This weekend I shall play with Huey.*

"That's a cute little puppy," Louise whispered.

"Huey's my rescue puppy," Hannah said proudly. "I chose him at Battersea Dogs & Cats Home. He's coming home today!" She glanced at the paper in front of Louise.

On it were the words: *I am going to Gemma's birthday party picnic in Battersea Park,* and a picture of a birthday cake.

"You're coming tomorrow, aren't you?" Louise whispered. "Everyone in the class has been invited."

Hannah glanced at Gemma in the back row. Gemma narrowed her eyes at her. Hannah shook her head sadly.

"Gemma hasn't invited me," she sighed.

"Well, *I* have!" Louise said. "I think you and Gemma

should be friends. It's not fair to leave you out when all the class has been invited . . ." Louise looked thoughtful. "I know!" She grinned cheekily. "Bring Huey, then Gemma will think you were just taking him for a walk in the park!"

"I'm not sure that's a good idea . . ." Hannah began, but she was interrupted by the bell for the end of school.

"Have a great weekend, everyone!" Miss Reynolds told Year Three Acorns as Hannah joined the dash out of the classroom door.

Hannah's heart thumped wildly as she waited at the school gates. There was no sign of Mum. Surely she and Dad had got Huey home by now. Why was she late, today of all days?

Huey Takes Them Home

Suddenly, a husky puppy appeared
round the corner. Huey ran towards
Hannah as fast as his little legs would
carry him. He was dragging something
behind him.

"Huey!" Hannah dashed towards
him as Mum screeched round
the corner, holding tight to
the end of the lead.

"Sorry we're late!" Mum panted, while
Huey greeted Hannah with a waggy tail
and slobbery licks. "We got caught in
traffic coming back from Battersea," she
explained, "so I thought I'd walk Huey to
school so he could stretch his legs. But
Huey decided to sniff every tree on
the way."

"Never mind, you're here!" Hannah
dropped to her knees
and threw her
arms around
Huey. "You're
my new best
friend," she
whispered into
his silky ears.
She wished
some of her
class were around
to see her with her new
puppy, but they'd all rushed off home.

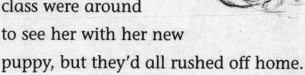

"Can I take Huey's lead?" she asked
Mum.

"We'll hold onto it together," Mum
said. "Huey's so strong, I'm afraid he'll
pull it out of your hand and run off if
you take him on your own."

"Time to go home, Huey." Hannah grabbed the lead just below Mum's hand at the exact same time as Huey spotted a cat in one of the front gardens next to the school. There was a hard tug on the lead and he launched himself after it.

"Now we know what it feels like to be on a sledge pulled along by a team of huskies!" Mum giggled as they held on tight, digging their heels into the pavement to slow Huey's headlong dash.

"It'd be awesome on snow and ice!"
Hannah laughed.

Mum stopped giggling. "It would be
dangerous!" she said seriously. "We
should be walking Huey like responsible
dog owners, not letting Huey walk *us*,"
she told Hannah as they pulled Huey
back to their side.

Huey looked up at them, panting and
wagging his tail. It was impossible to be
cross with him.

"Sit, Huey!"
Hannah pushed his
bottom down so
he was sitting.
"Good boy!" she
told him. "Now,
let's try again."

Hannah and
Mum gripped
Huey's lead.

"That's much better!" Hannah said
delightedly as Huey trotted along beside
them on his clumsy-looking
fluffy puppy feet.

"It'll be OK when Huey get used to us, and he knows we're in charge," Mum agreed. "You should practise walking him round and round the garden, where he can't run off. Then we can take him for a proper walk in Battersea Park . . ."

"Battersea Park!" Hannah exclaimed, remembering. "Gemma in my class is having a birthday picnic in Battersea

Park tomorrow!
Louise says I
should go along,
but I haven't
been invited."
Hannah
sighed. "All
the rest of the
class are going,
though."

Mum glanced
at her, looking
concerned.
"Gemma's mum
probably didn't give her enough
invitations," she said slowly. "I don't
expect she even knew that you'd joined
Acorn Class. I'll call her. Her number is
on the class contact list Miss Reynolds
gave me."

And before Hannah could stop her,
Mum one-handedly
rummaged in her
handbag, whipped
out the class list
and her mobile
phone, and called
Gemma's mum.
Hannah's cheeks
burned as Mum
explained that she was sure
Hannah had been
accidentally left out
of the invitations to
Gemma's birthday
party picnic.

Mum snapped
the phone shut
with a satisfied
look on her face.

"Gemma's mum is very sorry you were missed out," she told Hannah. "It's fine for you to go to the picnic. The more the merrier, she says. I checked the time and place. It'll be a great chance for you to get to know everyone better, won't it?"

"Great," Hannah said, trying to sound enthusiastic. She didn't want to tell Mum that she thought Gemma had left her out deliberately. But there was no time to worry about it. They were home!

Home Sweet Home

"Here we are, Huey," Hannah said,
opening the garden gate and carefully
shutting it behind them. "This is where
we live. This is home now!" She bent
down and unclipped Huey's lead.

Ooooh! The little husky puppy howled
a tiny joyful howl and raced madly
around the garden, sniffing
enthusiastically.

Hannah could
tell he was overjoyed
to be running free.
"I'll get your ball." Hannah
dashed inside and grabbed Huey's
new toy. From the window, she could
see Ellie opening the garden gate.
Hannah watched as Huey raced up and
jumped joyfully around Ellie. She smiled
as Ellie put down her school bag and

bent to tickle him
behind the ears.
Huey was
melting her
big sister's
heart too.

"I'm going to
teach him how to
fetch!" Hannah
informed Ellie. "Want to join in?" And
before Ellie could say "no" she tossed the
squeaky ball to Ellie. Ellie threw it back to

her. Huey bounced up
and down on all
fours with
excitement.
"Fetch!"
Hannah
ordered, throwing
the ball for Huey.

The little husky puppy shot after the ball and grabbed it, but he didn't bring it back. He just raced round and round in circles on the long grass. Hannah chased after him. He was so fast, he was hard to catch.

"Let me have a go," Ellie giggled as Hannah rugby-tackled Huey and gently prised the squeaky ball out of his jaws. It was covered in doggy dribble. Hannah threw it to her sister.

"Ugh!" Ellie shrieked, dropping the slimy ball in disgust. Huey pounced on it with glee and raced off with it again. Hannah looked on in  amazement as Ellie dashed after him, forgetting for once that she was cool.

"I'm puffed out," Ellie gasped, after they'd been playing for half an hour.

"Me, too," Hannah panted, "but Huey's as fresh as a daisy."

"Huskies are famous for their stamina," Mum laughed, bringing out a jug of lemonade. "They can pull sledges for hours on end. It takes an awful lot to tire them out." Hannah glugged down her lemonade and went inside to fetch Huey's water bowl. Huey lapped at the water with his bright pink tongue. Then he sat down at Hannah's feet and looked expectantly at her.

"He must be hungry," Mum said. "I'll fetch his dinner." She returned with a bowl of dried dog food. Huey wolfed it down and took another drink.

"Time for walking practice, Huey," Hannah told him, clipping the lead back onto his collar. Huey

trotted obediently next to her as she walked him round and round the garden.

"Look at us!" she called to Mum and Ellie. "Huey's walking to heel! I can take him to Battersea Park tomorrow!"

"Well done, Huey and Hannah!" Mum whooped, and she and Ellie clapped.

At the sound of the clapping, Huey's tail wagged and wagged. Then all at once he sat down and gave an enormous yawn, showing his pointy little puppy

teeth. The next second, he'd curled up in
a ball next to
Hannah's feet,
and was fast
asleep.

"At last!"
Mum
laughed.

"Huey's
had a big
day for such
a little
puppy," Hannah
said, picking him up
and carrying him into the house. She
lovingly placed him in his new basket
and put his squeaky bone next to him.
Puppy snores echoed around the kitchen.

Hannah sat on the floor next to Huey
and softly stroked his head as he slept.

It was awesomely, amazingly brilliant to have her very own puppy! For the first time, Hannah felt really at home in the new house – and it was easy to tell that Huey did, too. He was wagging his tail in his sleep!

The Birthday Party Surprise

"Hannah! Time to go to Battersea Park for Gemma's party," Mum called. "Don't forget the poo bags!"

"They're in my backpack, Mum!" Hannah's tummy felt as if it was full of butterflies. Huey was too young to manage the stairs on his own, so he scooped him up in her arms, shut her bedroom door and carefully carried him downstairs. They'd been having fun playing a game of hide-and-squeak with the squeaky bone in her bedroom, and the whole room was a terrible mess.

Hannah carefully set Huey down and picked up a small box that she'd left by the front door. It was covered in pictures of cute dogs.

"When I went to the supermarket with Grandpa, I bought this with my pocket money," she told Mum. "Do you think Gemma would like it for her birthday?"

Mum peered into the box and smiled.
"I think she'll love it."

"Good!" Hannah breathed a sigh of
relief as she popped the box into her
backpack. *I hope Gemma will be pleased to
see me*, she thought.

Hannah clipped the lead onto Huey's
collar and led him out to the car. He sat
on an old towel on the back seat next to
her and gazed out of the car window
as they drove along. In no time at
all, the window was covered
in puppy-breath nose
prints.

"It's a lovely warm, sunny day for a picnic," Mum commented, opening the car windows a crack. Huey sniffed deeply and pricked up his furry ears.

Wooo-ooo, he howled.

"What is it, Huey?" Hannah asked.

"He can smell his old home," Mum told her. "We must be very close to Battersea Dogs & Cats Home."

"You've moved house, Huey," Hannah told him. "Just like us!" Huey stopped howling and licked Hannah's hand. The end of his tail twitched happily.

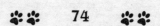

Mum parked the car near Albert Bridge and put money in the parking meter. "The party's at the adventure playground," she said, glancing at her watch. "We're right on time."

Sure enough, a group of Hannah's classmates and their parents were gathered at the picnic tables outside the playground. Hannah spotted Louise amongst them.

"You take Huey, and I'll go and talk to the other mums," Mum said in a low voice. "Good luck, love!"

Hannah took a deep breath, and walked towards Louise. Huey trotted at her heels. He was behaving perfectly!

"Hannah!" Louise ran towards her, smiling broadly. "That's the coolest puppy ever!"

Huey gazed up at Louise with his big blue eyes. His tail wagged.

"Can I stroke him?" Louise asked.

"Of course," Hannah told her, with a smile.

One by one the members of Acorn Class surrounded them. They bombarded Hannah with questions.

"Is he a wolf?"

"Can he pull sledges?"

"Where did you get him from?"

Hannah
answered as
well as she
could. Huey
licked
everyone's
hands and
wagged his
tail furiously
while all the
children petted
and admired him.

"He thinks he's part of the pack and
he's loving it," Hannah giggled. *She*
was too!

"Hey, Gemma!"
Louise called across the
adventure playground.
"Come and meet
someone special!"

Gemma slid down the slide and raced over to see what all the fuss was about. She stopped dead when she spotted Hannah's head in the crowd.

"What are you doing here?" she hissed. "I didn't invite you to my party!"

Hannah's face fell. "Your mum said I could come," she murmured. "I just wanted to make friends," she said, glancing at Louise.

"Louise isn't your friend, she's *my* friend," Gemma thundered. "And it's *my* birthday party, and I don't want you or your puppy here!"

Gemma flounced back into the adventure playground, reluctantly followed by the rest of her classmates. Louise hung back, looking embarrassed.

Hannah could feel the tears welling up in her eyes. Why did Gemma hate her so much? She didn't want to take Louise away from her. Why couldn't they all be friends?

Huey's tail was
drooping, too, as he
watched the
children playing
without him.
He sat down
and raised his
muzzle into the air.
Wooo-ooo, he howled.

"We have to go home, Huey," Hannah
said, pulling on his lead.

Huey refused to budge. Hannah gave
a tug on his lead.
Huey's collar
slipped over his
head and,
before Hannah
could do
anything about
it, he raced off.

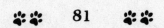

Hannah was left with the empty collar dangling from his lead. It must have come loose with all the petting. Hannah burst into tears. Now she had no new friends and her puppy had run away!

A Whole New Pack of Friends

Louise hurried back and put her arm round Hannah's shoulders.

"Huey hasn't gone far," she said. "Look!"

Hannah wiped the tears from her eyes and turned to see where Louise was pointing. There was Huey, standing at the bottom of a big wide slide, wagging his

long tail as Gemma and her friends
slithered down it. The instant Gemma
landed, Huey rushed up to her and
covered her in sloppy licks.

"Geddoff!" Gemma spluttered as
Hannah and Louise raced
towards her. But Gemma's
squeals began to turn
into peals of
laughter.

"I'm sorry," Hannah murmured as she pulled Huey off Gemma and re-fastened his collar around his neck. "He got away."

Huey sat down and looked innocently at them. He was panting a bit and his eyes were twinkling.

"Awww, he's so cute!" Gemma giggled, dropping to her knees and giving Huey a big hug.

She looked up
sheepishly at
Hannah.

"I'd really
like it if Huey
could stay for
my party!"
Gemma told
Hannah.

Louise coughed
and put her hands on her hips.

"And I'd like you to stay too, of
course," Gemma said, with
a friendly smile.

"Thanks!" An enormous grin lit up Hannah's face. "I've got a present for you." She rummaged in her backpack. "Happy birthday, Gemma!"

Gemma jumped to her feet and curiously opened the box. She took out a tiny cuddly toy dog.

"It's a husky!" she laughed. "Just like Huey! Thanks, Hannah, I love it! I'm sorry I was mean to you before . . ."

"Time for the birthday cake!" Gemma's mum yelled from the picnic table.

"Come and help me blow out the candles." Gemma put one arm around Hannah's shoulder and one around Louise's. Louise winked at Hannah and grinned from ear to ear.

Hannah could see her mum smiling with delight as the three girls made their way towards the picnic tables with Huey trotting along beside them.

"Hip, hip, hooray!" The mums led the cheering as Hannah and Louise helped Gemma blow out the candles on her birthday cake, watched by the rest of the class.

Wooo-ooo! Huey howled for joy. Everyone looked at him and laughed.

Hannah couldn't stop smiling. Her wonderful husky puppy had helped her make a whole pack of new friends!

Read on for lots more . . .

🐾 🐾 🐾 🐾

Battersea Dogs & Cats Home

Battersea Dogs & Cats Home is a charity that aims never to turn away a dog or cat in need of our help. We reunite lost dogs and cats with their owners; when we can't do this, we care for them until new homes can be found for them; and we educate the public about responsible pet ownership. Every year the Home takes in around 12,000 dogs and cats. In addition to the site in south-west London, the Home also has two other centres based at Old Windsor, Berkshire, and Brands Hatch, Kent.

The original site in Holloway

History

The Temporary Home for Lost and Starving Dogs was originally opened in a stable yard in Holloway in 1860 by Mary Tealby after she found a starving puppy in the street. There was no one to look after him, so she took him home and nursed him back to health. She was so worried about the other dogs wandering the streets that she opened the Temporary Home for Lost and Starving Dogs. The Home was established to help to look after them all and find them new homes.

Sadly Mary Tealby died in 1865, aged sixty-four, and little more is known about her, but her good work was continued. In 1871 the Home moved to its present site in Battersea, and was renamed the Dogs' Home Battersea.

Some important dates for the Home:

1883 – Battersea start taking in cats.

1914 – 100 sledge dogs are housed at the Hackbridge site, in preparation for Ernest Shackleton's second Antarctic expedition.

1956 – Queen Elizabeth II becomes patron of the Home.

2004 – Red the Lurcher's night-time antics become world famous when he is caught on camera regularly escaping from his kennel and liberating his canine chums for midnight feasts.

2007 – The BBC broadcast *Animal Rescue Live* from the Home for three weeks from mid-July to early August.

Amy Watson

Amy Watson has been working at
Battersea Dogs & Cats Home for six years
and has been the Home's Education
Officer for two and a half years. Amy's
role means that she organizes all the
school visits to the Home for children
aged sixteen and under, and regularly
visits schools around Battersea's three

sites to teach children how to behave and stay safe around dogs and cats, and all about responsible dog and cat ownership. She also regularly features on the Battersea website – www.battersea.org.uk – giving tips and advice on how to train your dog or cat under the "Amy's Answers" section.

On most school visits Amy can take a dog with her, so she is normally accompanied by her beautiful ex-Battersea dog Hattie. Hattie has been living with Amy for just over a year and really enjoys meeting new children and helping Amy with her work.

The process for re-homing a dog or a cat

When a lost dog or cat arrives, Battersea's Lost Dogs & Cats Line works hard to try to find the animal's owners. If, after seven days, they have not been able to reunite them, the search for a new home can begin.

The Home works hard to find caring, permanent new homes for all the lost and unwanted dogs and cats.

Dogs and cats have their own characters and so staff at the Home will spend time getting to know every dog and cat. This helps them decide the type of home the dog or cat needs.

There are five stages of the re-homing process at Battersea Dogs & Cats Home. Battersea's re-homing team wants to find you the perfect pet, sometimes this can take a while, so please be patient while we search for your new friend!

1 Application

2 Interview

3 Home visit

4 Searching for a pet

5 Leaving with your new pet

Have a look at our website:
http://www.battersea.org.uk/dogs/ rehoming/index.html for more details!

"Did you know?" questions about dogs and cats

- Puppies do not open their eyes until they are about two weeks old.

- According to *The Guinness Book of Records*, the smallest living dog is a long-haired Chihuahua called Danka Kordak from Slovakia, who is 13.8cm tall and 18.8cm long.

- Dalmatians, with all those cute black spots, are actually born white.

- The greyhound is the fastest dog on earth. It can reach speeds of up to 45 miles per hour.

- The first living creature sent into space was a female dog named Laika.

- Cats spend 15% of their day grooming themselves and a massive 70% of their day sleeping.

- Cats see six times better in the dark than we do.

- A cat's tail helps it to balance when it is on the move – especially when jumping.

- The cat, giraffe and camel are the only animals that walk by moving both their left feet, then both their right feet, when walking.

Dos and Don'ts of looking after dogs and cats

Dogs dos and don'ts

DO

- Be gentle and quiet around dogs at all times – treat them as you would like to be treated.
- Have respect for dogs.

DON'T

- Sneak up on a dog – you could scare them.
- Tease a dog – it's not fair.
- Stare at a dog – dogs can find this scary.
- Disturb a dog who is sleeping or eating.

- Assume a dog wants to play
  with you. Just like you,
  sometimes they may want to
  be left alone.
- Approach a dog who is without
  an owner as you won't know if
  the dog is friendly or not.

Cats dos and don'ts

DO
- Be gentle and quiet around
  cats at all times.
- Have respect for cats.
- Let cats approach you in their
  own time.

DON'T
- Never stare at a cat as they
  can find this intimidating.

- Tease a cat – it's not fair.
- Disturb a sleeping or eating cat – they may not want attention or to play.
- Assume a cat will always want to play. Like you, sometimes they want to be left alone.

Here is a delicious recipe for you to follow.

Remember to ask an adult to help you.

Cheddar Cheese Dog Cookies

You will need:

227g grated Cheddar cheese

(use at room temperature)

114g margarine

1 egg

1 clove of garlic (crushed)

172g wholewheat flour

30g wheatgerm

1 teaspoon salt

30ml milk

Preheat the oven to 375°F/190°C/gas mark 5.

Cream the cheese and margarine together.

When smooth, add the egg and garlic and

mix well. Add the flour, wheatgerm and salt. Mix well until a dough forms. Add the milk and mix again.

Chill the mixture in the fridge for one hour.

Roll the dough onto a floured surface until it is about 4cm thick. Use cookie cutters to cut out shapes.

Bake on an ungreased baking tray for 15–18 minutes.

Cool to room temperature and store in an airtight container in the fridge.

Some fun pet-themed puzzles!

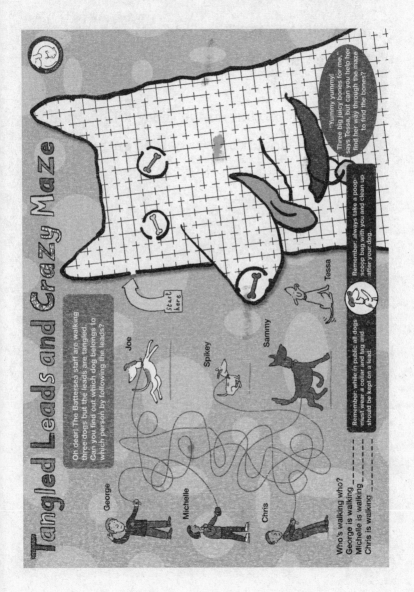

What a dog needs!

Here is a list of things that a dog needs for a long, happy and healthy life. See if you can find them in the word search and while you look, think why they might be so important. The words could be written backwards, diagonally, forwards, up and down so look carefully and GOOD LUCK!

FOOD   COLLAR
WATER   LEAD
TREATS   BED
TOYS   EXERCISE
VET CARE   TRAINING
GROOMING   LOVE
RESPONSIBLE OWNERS

Remember don't disturb a dog especially if it is sleeping or eating

Can you think of any other things a dog may need? Write them in the spaces below.

110

Drawing dogs and cats

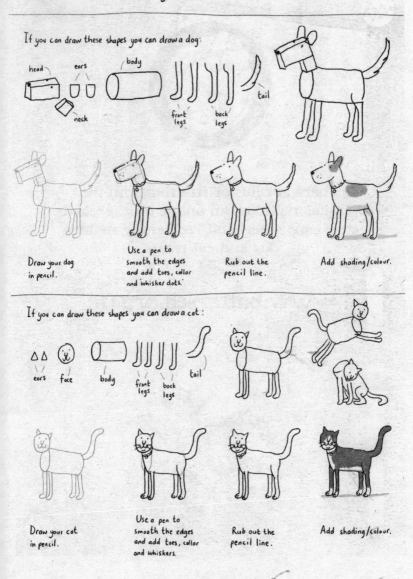

If you can draw these shapes you can draw a dog:

head   ears   body   front legs   back legs   tail   neck

Draw your dog in pencil.

Use a pen to smooth the edges and add toes, collar and whisker dots.

Rub out the pencil line.

Add shading/colour.

If you can draw these shapes you can draw a cat:

ears   face   body   front legs   back legs   tail

Draw your cat in pencil.

Use a pen to smooth the edges and add toes, collar and whiskers.

Rub out the pencil line.

Add shading/colour.

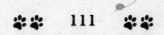

There are lots of fun things on the website, including an online quiz, e-cards, colouring sheets and recipes for making dog and cat treats.

www.battersea.org.uk